Forever in Your Heart

Katie Zapfel

Illustrated by
Amara Venayas Rodriguez

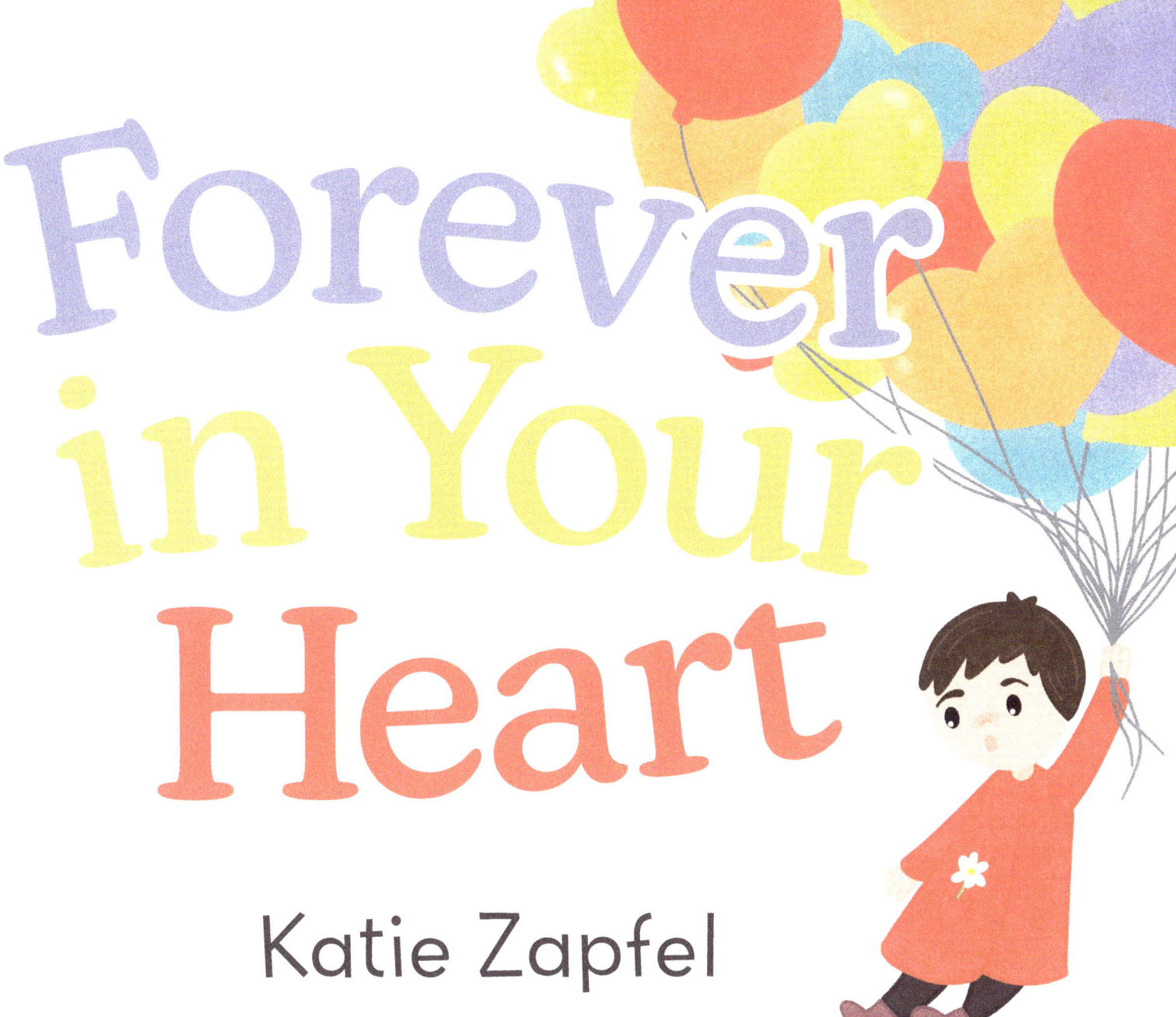

Published by Orange Hat Publishing 2022
ISBN 9781645383482

Copyrighted © 2022 by Katie Zapfel
All Rights Reserved
Forever in Your Heart
Written by Katie Zapfel
Illustrated by Amara Venayas Rodriguez

This publication and all contents within may not be reproduced or transmitted in any part or in its entirety without the written permission of the author.

www.orangehatpublishing.com

To Leo, Finn, and Noah

If ever I am far,
Far away from you,
I'd swim an ocean wide and blue
To get back home to you.

And up above the clouds, so high,
Together we would run.

To light you on your way, sweet one,
No distance would be too far.

And if someday there was someone
Who ever let you down,
I'll be the breeze that rustles the trees
And carries you safe to ground.

And if ever you are sad, my dear,
Remember one thing is true:
Anywhere you rest your head,
I'll be right there with you.

Because there is nothing
                    like the 'you and me'

That we will always be,

So if you ever miss me, my love,
On the days we spend apart,
Remember that I am always
Forever in your heart.

CPSIA information can be obtained
at www.ICGtesting.com
Printed in the USA
BVHW020721250422
634768BV00003B/3